Happy 3rd Birthday Henry

Love + Kisses

Sharon xxx

Francesca Simon

DON'T BE HORRID, HENRY

Illustrated by Kevin McAleenan

TED SMART

For Judith Elliott...
probably the world's best editor

First published in 2000 by
Orion Children's Books
a division of the Orion Publishing Group Ltd
Orion House
5 Upper St Martin's Lane
London WC2H 9EA

This edition produced for
The Book People Ltd
Hall Wood Avenue, Haydock
St Helens WA11 9UL

Printed and bound in Italy by Printer Trento S.r.l.

Henry was a horrid baby.

He screamed
in the morning.

He screamed
in the evening.

At night
he never slept.

He put breakfast
on his head,

lunch
on the floor,

dinner
on the walls.

And his nappies … what a stink!

Then Peter was born.

Peter was a perfect baby. He smiled all day and slept all night.
His nappies were never dirty (well, almost never).

Henry was not very happy when Peter arrived. In fact, he was furious.
"I've had just about enough of this baby," he said to Mum.
"Gootchie gootchie goo," said Mum.

"Time to take that baby back to the hospital," he said to Dad.
"Who's my little plumpikins?" said Dad.

Henry glared at Peter. This house isn't big enough for both of us, he thought.

Horrid Henry tried posting Peter.

He tried dumping Peter.

He tried losing Peter.

He tried letting the wind blow him away.

Perhaps he'll leave, thought Horrid Henry hopefully.

Unfortunately, Peter didn't. He just grew bigger and bigger, sitting in Henry's chair, playing with Henry's toys, swinging on Henry's swing, and being a total nuisance.

"Mum! Peter's kicking me!" screamed Henry.

"Don't be a tell-tale, Henry!"

"Dad! Peter's bashing my teddy!"

"He's only little, Henry!"

"Mum! Henry's hitting me!" said Peter.

"Don't be horrid, Henry!"

"Dad! Henry's knocking down my Lego!"

"Don't be horrid, Henry!"

"Why doesn't Peter ever get into trouble?" muttered Henry.

Then Horrid Henry had a wonderful, wicked idea.

"Peter," said Henry sweetly, "would you like to dig a hole to China?"
"Oh yes," said Peter.
Henry pointed to Mum's newly-dug flower-bed.
"Dig here," he said. "It's easier."

Peter started digging. Soon there was a lovely big hole.
"That's great work, Peter," said Henry. "Why not show Mum?"
Peter toddled off.

Tee hee, thought Horrid Henry.

Mum came outside.

"AARGGHHH!" she screamed.

"Henry! How dare you dig up my flower-bed!"

"I didn't do it," said Henry. "Peter did."

"Don't be horrid, Henry!" shouted Mum.
"Go to your room!"
"It's not fair!" wailed Henry.
 Next day, he tried again.

"Let's surprise Mum and draw her a beautiful picture," said Henry.
"How about a Viking ship?"
"Yeah!" said Peter.
"We need a huge space," said Henry. "I know! Let's draw on the wall!"
"On the wall?" said Peter.
"We couldn't fit a whole Viking ship on a tiny piece of paper," said
    Henry. "And just think how pleased Mum will be when she sees it."

"Okay," said Peter.

Henry giggled and sneaked off. This time *he'd* get Mum himself.

"Mum, Mum, Peter's doing something terrible!"
said Horrid Henry. "He's drawing on the walls!"

Mum ran upstairs.

"I didn't do it, my hand did," said Peter. "It was Henry's idea."

"No it wasn't!"

"Don't be horrid, Henry!" shouted Mum.

"But I didn't do anything!" said Henry.

"You're the eldest! You should have stopped him," said Mum.

"Go to your room!"

The next day Mum took Henry and Peter to the park. Henry felt very sad. He couldn't get rid of Peter, and he couldn't get Peter into trouble.

Maybe he could push Peter into a puddle when Mum wasn't looking.

Suddenly a huge dog ran up to Peter.
"GRRRRRRRR!" snarled the dog.
"Help!" squeaked Peter.
Henry didn't stop to think.
"GO AWAY, DOG!" he howled
   in his most horrid voice.

Peter started screaming.
Mum ran up.
"Don't be horrid, Henry!"
she shouted.

"Henry's not horrid," said Peter. "He saved me."

"My hero!" said Mum.

Henry allowed his mother to hug and kiss him.

He supposed he was happy to be a hero for a day.

But tomorrow – *watch out!*